P9-CPZ-138

by Tessa Krailing
illustrated by Mike Phillips

Editor: Jill Kalz
Page Production: Brandie Shoemaker
Art Director: Nathan Gassman
Associate Managing Editor: Christianne Jones

First American edition published in 2007 by
Picture Window Books
5115 Excelsior Boulevard
Suite 232
Minneapolis, MN 55416
877-845-8392
www.picturewindowbooks.com

This Americanization of DISGUSTING DENZIL was originally published in English in 2002 under the title DISGUSTING DENZIL by arrangement with Oxford University Press.

Printed in the United States of America.

Library of Congress Cataloging-in-Publication Data
Krailing, Tessa, 1935–
Disgusting Denzil / by Tessa Krailing ; illustrated by Mike Phillips.
p. cm. — (Read-it! chapter books)
Summary: When his baby sister arrives and nobody pays attention to Denzil anymore, he is ready to run away from home, until he discovers how proud he is to have a sister who is the most disgusting monster around.
ISBN-13: 978-1-4048-3117-9 (library binding)
ISBN-10: 1-4048-3117-7 (library binding)
[1. Monsters—Fiction. 2. Babies—Fiction. 3. Brothers and sisters—Fiction.]
I. Phillips, Mike, 1961– ill. II. Title.
PZ7.K85855Di 2006
[Fic]—dc22 2006027264

Table of Contents

Chapter One

"Oh, Denzil!" cried Denzil's mom, when he flicked fried chicken bits—SPLAT!—at her best dress.

"Denzil, you're disgusting!" said his dad, when Denzil squirted ketchup—GLOOP!—over the table.

And then both parents smiled quite fondly at their son.

Denzil felt proud. He knew he was disgusting. People often told him so.

"Denzil, you're the most disgusting monster in Monster City," they said.

Every morning, Denzil stared happily at himself in the mirror.

His hair was spiky, his nose ran, and his mouth dribbled.

No wonder his mom and dad adored him.

No wonder Miss Peabody, his teacher, gave him lots of stars.

Without a doubt, Denzil was everyone's favorite little monster ... until the day when it all began to go very, very wrong.

It started like any other day, with a really mucky, yucky breakfast.

Denzil managed to get it all over everything in the kitchen.

"Good shot!" said Dad, taking a glob of oatmeal from his left eye.

"Another winner!" exclaimed Mom. She picked up the piece of toast Denzil had dropped, jelly side down, on the floor.

Denzil smiled proudly.

Suddenly, Mom turned pale.

"Donovan," she said. (Donovan was the name of Denzil's dad.) "Donovan, would you fetch my suitcase? Quickly, please!"

Denzil didn't ask why his mother wanted her suitcase in the middle of breakfast. He was much too busy slurping up his milk—slurp, slurp, guzzle, BURP!

"Hey! Did you hear that, Mom?" he asked.

But Denzil's mom didn't tell him how clever he was, like she usually did. She just said, "Hurry off to school now, Denzil." And she pushed him out of the house, without even kissing him goodbye.

Puzzled, Denzil hurriedly made his way to school.

There, to his relief, things got better again. The first class was Yucky Jokes. Denzil told a joke about a monster who sat on a plate of moldy cheese. The other little monsters rolled on the floor with laughter.

"Oh, Denzil," said Miss Peabody. "That was the most disgusting joke I've ever heard!" She gave him four red stars, the highest mark a monster student could get.

The rest of the day wasn't bad, either. During art class, students had to do a self-portrait. "That means you have to paint yourself," said Mr. Boggis, the art teacher.

So Denzil painted himself all over in red and yellow stripes.

During music class, he blew his nose so loudly that everyone thought it was a foghorn.

Yes, it was a very good day … until Denzil went home, and Dad told him he had a new baby sister.

Chapter Two

Her name was Devora.

Dad took Denzil to see his new sister at the hospital. She lay in a crib beside Mom's bed. "Come and look at her," said Mom. "Little Devora. Isn't she sweet?"

The baby had a bald head, a scarlet face, a blobby nose, and screwed-up eyes. Denzil did think she looked rather sweet, but he wasn't going to say so.

Mom and Dad were gazing at her and making silly goo-goo noises.

"Who's Daddy's pride and joy?" cooed Dad.

Pride and joy? Denzil was shocked and hurt. That's what Dad had always called him. But the baby had done nothing to deserve such praise.

Devora just lay there like a—well, like a baby.

Suddenly, she yawned—a yawn so enormous that Denzil quickly stepped back.

The baby's mouth was like a deep, red cavern.

Denzil had never seen a mouth so huge. It seemed twice the size of the rest of Devora's body. But when she shut it again, it looked quite normal.

"Give her to me," said Mom. "I want to hold her."

Gently, Dad lifted the baby out of the crib. He placed her in Mom's arms. The baby opened her eyes and smiled. Then she spit up a whole lot of white stuff.

"What a clever girl!" cried Dad. "I think she's going to be even more disgusting than Denzil."

A cold, clammy fear took hold of Denzil. He stared at his baby sister.

Devora dribbled and coughed. Then she yawned again, showing her toothless gums in an awesome display of disgustingness. Was she really going to be worse than him?

"My baby," said Mom tenderly.

Chapter Three

From the moment Devora came home from the hospital, Denzil's life changed. The baby was the only thing anybody wanted to look at.

"Isn't she amazing!" they cried. "Isn't she gorgeous!"

Nobody paid any attention to Denzil—no one.

Devora put on a real show for them. At her top end, she was really disgusting, forever drooling and burping. But she was even more disgusting at her bottom end. Well, it's probably better not to say what happened at her bottom end. Even Denzil had to admit that it was far more disgusting than anything he could do.

"Denzil, would you like to hold your baby sister?" offered Mom.

"No, thanks," he said.

"Go on. Take her," said Mom. "She won't hurt you."

She put the baby into his arms.

Denzil stared down at Devora. Devora stared up at Denzil. Then she opened her mouth and screamed.

When Devora screamed, it was worse than when she yawned.

She made the most terrible noise, and her mouth was so huge that you could see right down to her stomach.

At least, that's how it seemed to poor Denzil.

He was scared. He was so scared that he wanted to run away. But he couldn't. He just sat there, staring into the large red hole that was Devora's mouth.

Mom laughed and said, "Oh dear, I think she's got a dirty diaper. Denzil, you can help me change her."

Denzil was stunned into silence. When it came to disgustingness, Devora beat him every time.

How would he ever make people notice him again?

Denzil went back outside. His plan had failed. Once again, Devora had beaten him.

What next?

At the back of the yard was a pond. It was a truly mucky pond, full of weeds and stinking slime. Denzil drew a deep breath and waded in with all of his clothes on.

Then he waded out again. He stood on the bank, dripping wet and covered in smelly, green slime.

Disgusting!

Proudly, he went indoors. "Look at me. I fell in the water," he said.

This wasn't true. But he didn't want to admit that he had walked into the pond on purpose.

Dad sniffed the air. "What's that lovely smell?" he asked.

Denzil puffed out his chest. "It's me!" he boasted.

"No, it's Devora," said Mom. "Her diaper needs changing again."

Denzil's shoulders sagged with disappointment.

At that moment, Devora saw him. She smiled and held out her arms.

"Oh, the little dear!" said Mom. "Your sister wants you to pick her up, Denzil."

"I don't think it's Denzil she wants," said Dad. "It's that fish poking out of his pocket."

Denzil looked down. Sure enough, there was a large, slippery, slithery fish sticking out of his pocket. It must have gotten stuck there while he was wading through the pond.

Denzil pulled it out.

Devora chuckled with delight. She got up from the floor and staggered toward him.

"Her first steps!" cried Mom.

"Give her the fish, Denzil," said Dad. "She deserves a reward."

But Denzil didn't have time to give her the fish. She had already snatched it out of his hands. In a split second, Devora opened her huge mouth and dropped the slimy, slippery fish inside.

Then she snapped her mouth shut and swallowed hard.

Denzil couldn't speak. He had never felt so disgusted in his life.

“Her first real food!” cried Dad. “She’s growing up fast. She’ll be talking next.”

Denzil’s heart sank to the bottom of his squishy boots. Every time he tried to be disgusting, Devora managed to be even more disgusting. It was hopeless. Nothing he could do would ever make his family admire him again.

Sadly, he turned around and walked out the front door.

Nobody even saw him go.

Chapter Five

Denzil trudged along the street.

"Hello, Denzil," Mrs. Wart called out. "I hear you have a new baby sister. Congratulations!"

Denzil couldn't even manage a smile. He shrugged and walked on.

"Hello, Denzil," Miss Peabody, his teacher, called out. "I hear your baby sister is growing up fast. She'll soon be ready to come to school."

Denzil opened his mouth to speak, but no sound came out. The thought of Devora coming to school was too awful. It was bad enough that she grabbed all of the attention at home. He dreaded having to compete with her at school, too. He shrugged and walked on.

"Denzil!" Sickening Susan, his classmate, called out. "You are so lucky, having a new baby sister. I wish I had one."

"You can have mine" was what Denzil wanted to say. But he didn't. He just shrugged and walked on. At last he came to the park.

He sat down on a bench.

Tears rolled down his cheeks. He was no longer the most disgusting little monster in Monster City, only the brother of the most disgusting little monster in Monster City.

Someone came to sit beside him. Denzil brushed away the tears.

It was Boastful Bertha. She was holding onto a stroller.

Not another baby! Denzil had had quite enough of babies, thanks very much. He got up to go.

"Look, Denzil," said Bertha. "This is my new baby brother. Isn't he totally disgusting?"

Denzil glanced at the baby in the stroller. He didn't think Bertha's brother was much to look at.

"He's not as disgusting as my baby sister," he said.

Bertha's brother spit up something revolting and green.

"Look at that," said Bertha. "He's been eating grass. I bet your baby sister doesn't eat grass."

“She eats fish,” said Denzil. “Raw.”

The baby screwed up his eyes and made a very rude noise.

“He’s got gas,” said Bertha. “I bet your baby sister doesn’t make noises like that.”

“When my baby sister has gas,” said Denzil, “everyone runs out in the street. They think there’s a war going on.”

The baby’s face turned red. He opened his mouth and screamed.

“I bet your baby sister can’t yell as loud as that,” said Bertha.

"When my baby sister yells," said Denzil, "you can hear her miles and miles away. And when she opens her mouth, it's so big you can see right down to her stomach. Her mouth is bigger than a shark's ... or even a whale's! I bet she could swallow a whole person if she wanted to."

Bertha stared at him. "That's impossible," she said.

Denzil shrugged. "Come over to my house and take a look," he said.

"When?" Bertha asked.

"Now," Denzil replied.

Denzil set off. Behind him, he heard the stroller wheels squeaking as Bertha followed him home.

"Hello, Mom," he called out as he opened the front door. "Can Boastful Bertha take a look at Devora?"

"Yes, of course," said Mom. "Is that your new baby brother, Bertha? My, isn't he disgusting!"

"He's not as disgusting as Devora," said Denzil. There was definitely a note of pride in his voice.

They entered the living room. A crowd was standing around Devora, gazing at her admiringly. They made way for Denzil and for Bertha, who was carrying her baby brother.

When Bertha's baby brother saw Devora, he opened his mouth wide and screamed.

Devora looked up in surprise.

Then she, too, opened her mouth and screamed.

Bertha turned pale.

Bertha's baby brother stopped screaming. He clutched her tightly. Bertha stared down at Devora's huge mouth. It was getting bigger and bigger with every scream—

BIGGER

AND BIGGER

AND BIGGER!

Bertha turned and fled.

As soon as the other baby left, Devora stopped screaming. She closed her mouth and smiled. She looked up at Denzil and said in a hoarse, booming voice, "Den—zil."

Everyone gasped.

"Listen to that!" cried Dad. "She said her first word."

"I knew it wouldn't be long before she started talking," said Mom, "the little dear."

Denzil nearly burst with pride. Devora was far, far more disgusting than Bertha's baby brother. And her first word had been his name.

"Den—zil," Devora said again, loudly and clearly. "Den—zil, Den—zil, Den—zil."

She held out her arms, waggling her short, fat fingers.

"Look at that," sighed everyone. "How she loves her big brother!"

Dad looked puzzled. "I think she wants something," he said.

Denzil smiled. "Slugs, I suppose," he said. "The others have all wriggled away. I'll go and get Devora some more."

Happily, he picked up a cardboard box and went into the garden.

Look for More *Read-it!* Chapter Books

The Badcat Gang
Beastly Basil
Cat Baby
Cleaner Genie
Clever Monkeys
Contest Crazy
Duperball
Elvis the Squirrel
Eric's Talking Ears
High Five Hank
Hot Dog and the Talent Competition
Nelly the Monstersitter
On the Ghost Trail
Scratch and Sniff
Sid and Bolter
Stan the Dog Becomes Superdog
The Thing in the Basement
Tough Ronald